JAMES

Based on *The Railway Series* by the Rev. W. Awdry

Illustrations by
Robin Davies and Creative Design

EGMONT

First published in Great Britain 2003
by Egmont Books Limited
239 Kensington High Street, London W8 6SA
All Rights Reserved

Thomas the Tank Engine & Friends

A BRITT ALLCROFT COMPANY PRODUCTION

Based on The Railway Series by The Rev W Awdry

ISBN 1 4052 0693 4
3 5 7 9 10 8 6 4
Printed in China

This is a story about James the Red Engine. When he first arrived on Sodor, he was so busy thinking about his shiny red paint that he soon got into lots of trouble. I thought I might have to send him away …

James was a new engine, with a shining coat of red paint. He had two small wheels in front and six driving wheels behind. They were smaller than Gordon's, but bigger than Thomas'.

"You're a special 'mixed traffic' engine," The Fat Controller told James. "That means you can pull either coaches or trucks."

James felt very proud.

The Fat Controller told James that today he was to help Edward pull coaches.

"You need to be careful with coaches," said Edward. "They don't like getting bumped. If you bump them, they'll get cross."

But James was thinking about his shiny red coat and wasn't really listening.

James and Edward took the coaches to the platform. A group of boys came over to admire James.

"I really am a splendid engine," thought James, and he let out a great *wheeeeeesh* of steam. Everyone jumped, and a shower of water fell on The Fat Controller, soaking his brand new top hat!

James thought he had better leave quickly before he got into trouble, so he pulled away from the platform.

"Slow down!" puffed Edward, who didn't like starting quickly.

"You're going too fast, you're going too fast," grumbled the coaches.

When James reached the next station, he shot past the platform. His Driver had to back up so the passengers could get off the train.
"The Fat Controller won't be pleased when he hears about this," his Driver said.

James and Edward set off again, and started to climb a hill. "It's ever so steep, it's ever so steep," puffed James.

At last they got to the top, and pulled into the next station. James was panting so much that he got hiccups, and frightened an old lady, who dropped all her parcels.

"Oh, dear. The Fat Controller will be even crosser, now!" thought James.

The next morning, The Fat Controller spoke to James very sternly. "If you don't learn to behave better, I shall take away your red coat and paint you blue!" he warned. "Now run along and fetch your coaches."

James felt cross. "A splendid red engine like me shouldn't have to fetch his own coaches," he muttered.

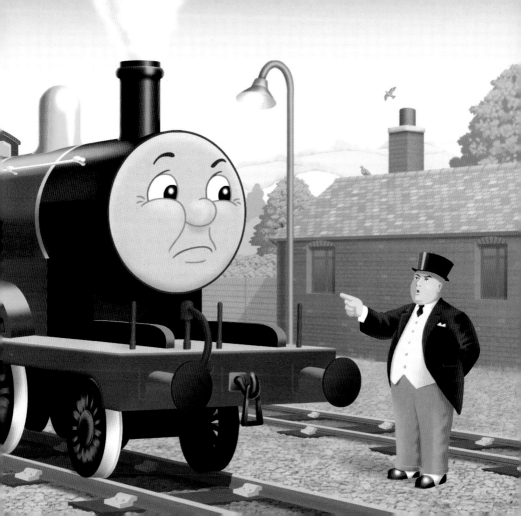

"I'll show them how to pull coaches," he said to himself, and he set off at top speed. The coaches groaned and protested as they bumped along. But James wouldn't slow down.

At last, the coaches had had enough. "We're going to stop, we're going to stop!" they cried, and try as he might, James found himself going slower and slower.

The Driver halted the train and got out. "There's a leak in the pipe," he said. "You were bumping the coaches hard enough to make a leak in anything!"

The Guard made all the passengers get out of the train. "You sir, please give me your bootlace," he said to one of them.

"No, I shan't!" said the passenger.

"Well then, we shall just have to stop where we are," said the Guard.

So the man agreed to give his bootlace to the Guard. The Guard used the lace to tie a pad of newspapers round the hole to stop the leak.

Now James was able to pull the train again. But he knew he was going to be in real trouble with The Fat Controller this time.

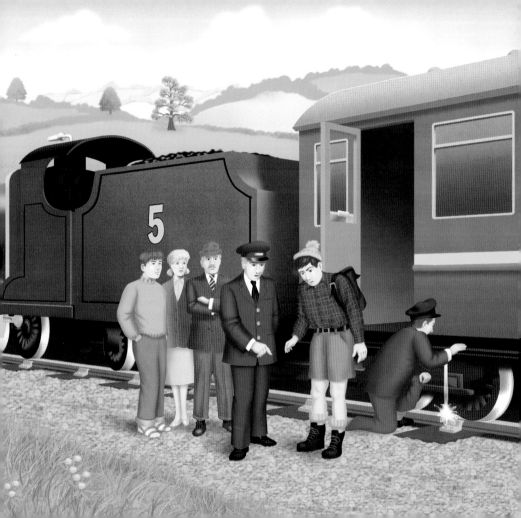

When James got back, The Fat Controller was very angry with him indeed.

For the next few days, James was left alone in the shed in disgrace. He wasn't even allowed to push coaches and trucks in the Yard.

He felt really sad.

Then one morning, The Fat Controller came to see him. "I see you are sorry," he said to James. "So I'd like you to pull some trucks for me."

"Thank you, sir!" said James, and he puffed happily away.

"Here are your trucks, James," said a little engine. "Have you got some bootlaces ready?" And he chuffed off, laughing rudely.

"Oh! Oh! Oh!" said the trucks as James backed down on them. "We want a proper engine, not a Red Monster."

James took no notice, but pulled the screeching trucks out of the Yard.

James started to heave the trucks up the hill, puffing and panting.

But halfway up, the last ten trucks broke away and rolled back down again. James' Driver shut off steam. "We'll have to go back and get them," he said to James.

James backed carefully down the hill to collect the trucks. Then with a 'peep peep' he was off again.

"I can do it, I can do it," he puffed, then… "I've done it, I've done it," he panted as he climbed over the top.

When James got back to the station, The Fat Controller was very pleased with him. "You've made the most Troublesome Trucks on the line behave," he said. "After that, you deserve to keep your red coat!"

James was really happy. He knew he was going to enjoy working on The Fat Controller's Railway!

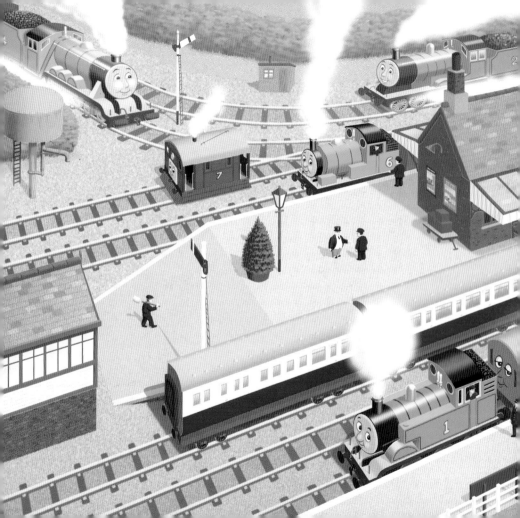

The Thomas Story Library is THE definitive collection of stories about Thomas and ALL his Friends.

You can buy the Collector's Pack containing the first ten books for £24.99!

ISBN 1 4052 0827 9

By the end of 2005, fifteen more Story Library titles will have chuffed into your local bookshop:

Gordon	**Henry**	**Trevor**
Edward	**Duck**	**Bertie**
Duncan	**Harold**	**Diesel**
Salty	**Peter Sam**	**Daisy**
Stepney	**Emily**	**Spencer**

And there are even more
Thomas Story Library books to follow later!
So go on, start your Thomas Story Library NOW!

A Fantastic Offer for Thomas the Tank Engine Fans!

Thomas

STICK
POUND
COIN
HERE

In every Thomas Story Library book like this one, you will find a special token. Collect 6 Thomas tokens and we will send you a brilliant Thomas poster, and a double-sided bedroom door hanger!
Simply tape a £1 coin in the space above, and fill out the form overleaf.

TO BE COMPLETED BY AN ADULT

To apply for this great offer, ask an adult to complete the coupon below
and send it with a pound coin and 6 tokens, to:
THOMAS OFFERS, PO BOX 7, MANCHESTER M19 2HD

☐ Please send a Thomas poster and door hanger. I enclose 6 tokens
plus a £1 coin. (Price includes P&P)

Fan's name...

Address...

....Postcode..........................

Date of birth...

Name of parent/guardian...

Signature of parent/guardian...

Please allow 28 days for delivery. Offer is only available while stocks last. We reserve the right to change
the terms of this offer at any time and we offer a 14 day money back guarantee. This does not affect your
statutory rights.

☐ Data Protection Act: If you do not wish to receive other similar offers from us or companies we
recommend, please tick this box. Offers apply to UK only.